Bye Bye Baby

Janet & Allan Ahlberg

PUFFIN

PUFFIN BOOKS

UK | USA | Canada | Ireland | Australia | India | New Zealand | South Africa

Puffin Books is part of the Penguin Random House group of companies
whose addresses can be found at global.penguinrandomhouse.com.

www.penguin.co.uk   www.puffin.co.uk   www.ladybird.co.uk

Penguin
Random House
UK

First published by William Heinemann Ltd 1989
Published by Puffin Books 1999
This edition published 2019

001

Copyright © Janet and Allan Ahlberg, 1989

The moral right of the author and illustrator has been asserted

Printed in China

A CIP catalogue record for this book is available from the British Library

ISBN: 978–0–241–38947–8

All correspondence to:
Puffin Books, Penguin Random House Children's
80 Strand, London WC2R 0RL

MIX
Paper from
responsible sources
FSC
www.fsc.org
FSC® C018179

BYE BYE BABY

Bye Bye Baby is probably my favourite example of Janet's work. The book, though, had a chequered life. It started out as one of a set (with another illustrator): *Robot Baby*, *Giant Baby*, *Jelly Baby*, etc. Rejected and left in a drawer for three or four years, it somehow got out and on to Janet's board. Afterwards, when the book was published, we spotted a mistake. The baby's beloved toy rabbit was not included in his packing (small suitcase on the half-title and elsewhere). For the paperback edition, Janet painted it in.

Allan Ahlberg

There was once a baby who had no mummy.
This baby lived in a little house all by himself.
He fed himself and bathed himself. He even
changed his own nappy.

It was very sad.

Then, one night, when the baby was putting himself to bed, he thought, 'I am too young to be doing this. I need a mummy!'

So, early the next morning, the baby left his little house – Bye-bye, baby! – and set off down the road to find a mummy. The baby could not walk far without resting. He could not walk fast without falling over. But he kept going just the same.

After a while the baby met a cat. This cat was sitting on a wall washing herself behind her ears.

'I am a little baby,' said the little baby, 'with no mummy. Will you be my mummy?'

'No, but I will be your cat,' said the cat, 'if you pour me a saucer of milk now and then. Also, I will help you find your mummy. She could pour me some milk too!'

So then the baby set off down the road – Bye-bye, baby! – with the cat beside him.

They had not gone far before they met a teddy. This teddy was sitting under a tree having a picnic.

'I am a little baby,' said the little baby, 'with no mummy. Will you be my mummy?'

'No, but I will be your teddy,' said the teddy, 'if you give me a cuddle once in a while. Also, I will help you find your mummy. She could be *my* mummy too!'

So then the baby set off down the road – Bye-bye, baby! – with the teddy and the cat beside him.

They had not gone far before they met a clockwork hen. This hen was scratching in the dirt at the side of the road and clucking to herself.

'I am a little baby,' said the little baby, 'with no mummy. Will you be my mummy?'

'Cluck, cluck!' said the hen, which meant, 'No, but I will be your clockwork hen, if you promise not to overwind me. Also, I will help you find your mummy. A mummy is a hen's best friend, so they say.'

So then the baby set off down the road – Bye-bye, baby! – with the clockwork hen and the teddy and the cat beside him.

They had not gone far before they met a grandpa. This grandpa was sitting on a bench reading a book.

'I am a little baby,' said the little baby, 'with no mummy. Will you be my mummy?'

'No, but I will be your grandpa,' said the grandpa, 'if you don't wake me up in the night. Also, I will help you find your mummy. Everyone needs his mummy – even me!'

So then the baby set off down the road – Bye-bye, baby! – with the grandpa and the clockwork hen and the teddy and the cat beside him.

They had not gone far . . .
before the trouble started.
The baby tripped over
and bumped his nose.

The teddy tripped over
and bumped *his*.

Both of them fell on the hen. The grandpa
tried to help, but only trod on the cat's tail.
Worst of all, the sky grew suddenly dark –
and it began to rain.

The baby sat on the ground (and also on the hen).

'*I want my mummy!*' he cried.

'He wants his mummy!' shouted the grandpa.

'Mummy!' shouted the cat and the teddy.

'Cluck!' which meant, 'Mummy!' shouted
the hen.

I want

Just then, round the corner came a lady pushing a pram. 'Did somebody call?' she said.

'I am a little baby,' cried the little baby, 'with *no* mummy!'

'There's a coincidence,' said the lady. 'I am a mummy with no little baby!'

'You could be made for each other,' said the grandpa.

Then the baby said, 'Will you be *my* mummy?'

And the mummy said, 'Yes!'

After that, the new mummy picked up her new baby, wiped the tears from his eyes and gave him a big kiss. With the rain falling faster, she put him in the pram and led the way up the road to her own little house.

As they hurried along, the teddy said, 'Will you
be my mummy too?' over and over again.
The cat said, 'Do you have any milk in your house?'
And the hen said, 'Cluck!' which this time just
meant 'Cluck'. She was still dazed from being sat on.

In the house the mummy gave the baby a warm
bath and a dry nappy. The grandpa made a pot
of tea. The teddy opened a packet of ginger biscuits.
All of them sat together in front of the fire.

The grandpa sipped his tea and turned
the pages of his book.

'Read us a story!' said the baby, as he
snuggled in his mummy's lap.

'What sort of story?' said the grandpa.

'A sad one,' said the cat.

'With a happy ending,' the mummy said.

'Right,' said the grandpa. Then – with the firelight flickering in the room, and the rain still rattling on the windows – he began to read.

'There was once a baby who had no . . . daddy!'

The baby's little eyes grew wide.

'I am a baby who has no daddy!' he said.

'There's another coincidence!' said the cat.

The baby clambered down from his mummy's knee and headed for the door.

'He's off to find a daddy!' the teddy said.

After that the baby set off down the road – Bye-bye, baby! – with his mummy and the grandpa and the teddy and the cat and the clockwork hen beside him.

And by and by
the baby met a horse.
   'Will you be my daddy?'

And by and by
the baby met a rabbit.
    'Will *you* be my daddy?'

And by and by
the baby met a *daddy*!
   'Will *YOU* be my daddy?'

And the daddy said . . .

The End